Starwhal

To Peter—keep sparkling!
M.R.

To my very own star, Julia
T.B.

The art in this book was created digitally.

Library of Congress Control Number 2020930139

ISBN 978-1-4197-4723-6

First published in 2020 by Hodder Children's Books, Hodder and Stoughton, London, U.K.
Original text copyright © 2020 Matilda Rose
Illustrations copyright © 2020 Tim Budgen
Book design by Katie Messenger
Cover design by Heather Kelly

Printed and bound in China
10 9 8 7 6 5 4 3 2

For bulk discount inquiries, contact specialsales@abramsbooks.com.

ABRAMS The Art of Books
195 Broadway, New York, NY 10007
abramsbooks.com

Starwhal

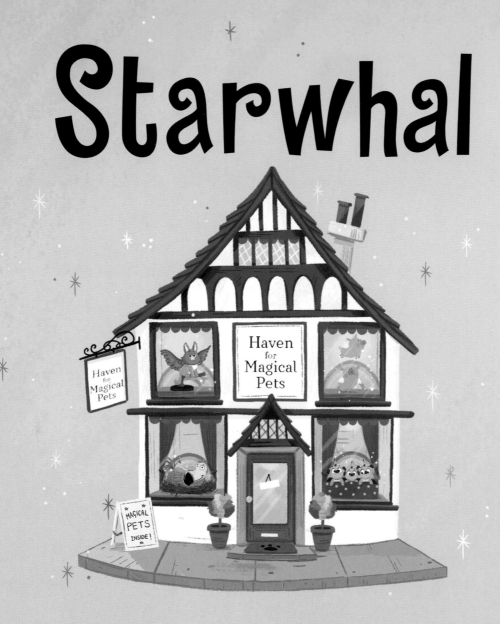

by **Matilda Rose** • illustrated by **Tim Budgen**

Abrams Appleseed
New York

Next time you're in Fairyland, make sure you visit Mrs. Paws's
Haven for Magical Pets in the town of Twinkleton-Under-Beanstalk.
It's a truly enchanting place. There are flying piglets,
cute baby griffins, and even pugicorns!

One day, Millie the Mermaid came
to the Haven for Magical Pets looking for
her perfect magical pet . . .

"Those cats look cuddly," said Millie.

But the cosmic cats did *not* like water!

The baby dragon was so cute.

But—*splash*—out went its flame!

And—*splosh*—the talking llamas were not impressed with their soggy new hairdos.

Would Millie ever find the right pet?

"Don't worry!" smiled Mrs. Paws. "I've just had a special arrival . . ."

It was a creature with big round eyes,
cute flappy flippers, and a long twisty horn.

"A narwhal!" gasped Millie.

"Almost!" laughed Mrs. Paws.

"This is a **Starwhal**. She's very rare. Just one touch from her magic horn will make anything sparkle!"

"Oh, I love her! Thank you!" said Millie.

"Starwhal's magic can do amazing things," said Mrs. Paws. "You just have to learn how to use it in the right way."

Back home in Coral Cove, Millie made sure
that Starwhal had everything she needed:
a comfy bed, toys to play with, and plenty
of delicious seapuffs to eat.

And she couldn't wait to try out
Starwhal's magical powers.

With a single touch of
Starwhal's horn . . .

Poof! The bed was
covered in sparkles.

Poof! The wardrobe
was full of twinkling,
glinting outfits.

Poof! Millie's whole bedroom was
transformed into a starry, shimmering wonderland!

"Please could you make my bubble-blower sparkly?" asked Millie's brother, Milo.

But Millie remembered what Mrs. Paws had said. She must use Starwhal's powers in the right way.

"No," said Millie. "I must only use Starwhal's magic for important things."

But later Millie couldn't
resist using a little more
of Starwhal's magic.

Poof! The Singing Rock
was all twinkly.

Poof! The seashell
path shimmered brightly.

Poof! Even Herman
the Crab was transformed!

And word soon spread
through Coral Cove . . .

"Could Starwhal please make
my mirror twinkly?" said Lola.
"No," said Millie. "Starwhal is *my* pet,
and I must use her magic wisely."

"What about my necklace?" asked Archie.

"Or my hair clip?" asked Pearl.

"Sorry, but I said no," huffed Millie.

But, back home, Millie decided to try out just a little more of Starwhal's magic for herself . . . and soon the whole house was glinting and gleaming!

It was so sparkly and pretty that Millie just *had* to show it off.
So she sent invitations to all of her friends:

You are invited to
a Starwhal Sparkle Party
Tomorrow at 3 p.m.
Seashell Cottage, Seahorse Walk,
Coral Cove
Love, Millie xoxo

Millie prepared an iced bubble cake and mixed up a jug of Seafruit Fizz.
Then she polished Starwhal's horn and put on her best necklace.
Then she waited . . . and waited . . .

but nobody came.

Millie's eyes felt hot and tickly. "Where is everyone?"
She sighed. "Come on, Starwhal—let's go and find them!"

Halfway through the coral reef, Millie and
Starwhal heard a funny *sniff–sniff* noise.

"Look! It's Prince Tristan!"
gasped Millie. "What's the matter?"

"I've—*sniff*—lost my—*sniff*—crown,"
Prince Tristan sobbed. "I'm supposed to be opening
the new Coral Cove Library this afternoon.
But how can I without my crown?!"

Just then, Starwhal flapped her flippers and her horn began to sparkle.

"Starwhal wants to help!" squealed Millie.

"I suppose we could use just a bit of magic . . ."

Millie picked some seaweed, braided it,
and—*poof!*—Starwhal transformed it
into a sparkling crown!

"Thank you!" said Tristan,
with a huge, happy smile. His smile
made Millie feel happy, too.

Mrs. Paws was right: Starwhal's
magic *could* do amazing things if
used in the right way!

Together, they swam to the library . . .

. . . just in time for the library's grand opening!

Tristan cut the ribbon, wearing his beautiful new crown.

And, to make the day extra special, Millie shared Starwhal's magic sparkle with everyone.

Coral Cove

Library

"I'm sorry," said Millie to her friends. "No one came to my party because I tried to keep Starwhal's magic for myself. But there is more than enough for us all!"